GEORGE ENNIS
JACKSON

JACKSON
Copyright © 2024 by George Ennis

ISBN: 979-8895311042 (sc)
ISBN: 979-8895311059 (e)

All rights reserved. No part of this publication may be reproduced, distributed, or transmitted in any form or by any means, including photocopying, recording, or other electronic or mechanical methods, without the prior written permission of the publisher and/or the author, except in the case of brief quotations embodied in critical reviews and other noncommercial uses permitted by copyright law.

The views expressed in this book are solely those of the author and do not necessarily reflect the views of the publisher, and the publisher hereby disclaims any responsibility for them.

Writers' Branding
(877) 608-6550
www.writersbranding.com
media@writersbranding.com

Once upon a time there was a very happy event. In the backyard a big mom rabbit gave birth to baby rabs. She had made her nest in an upside down orange crate, half hidden under dirt and packed with straw. It was the first part of February. Through a missing slat you could see this white ball of fur. If you looked very close at this ball, you could make out a pink ear, a closed eyelid, a foot with hairlike claws, and a pink nose which moved up and down with each tiny breath. Each day this rabbit ball got a little bigger and a little more active. A week went by and there was a lot of pushing when the mom entered her nest. You could see now where one baby stopped and another started. There were eight baby rabs; you could count them all. The ball would fall apart with so much kicking but it would quickly come together around the mom. Speaking of kicking, there was one ball rab that really kicked his brothers and sisters. This was a boy, of course, and he had huge hind feet. Everyone said he looked just like a jackrabbit, so they named him Jackson. This is a story about Jackson Rabbit.

When Jackson was a month old, he had many bad habits. He'd thump loudly on top of the box, and then with just two or three hops of his hind feet Jackson was off his box and half way across the yard. He could crack a carrot between his front teeth with an alarming noise. It was a big backyard all fenced in with a wire fence. There was a big tree right in the middle. Jackson ran in crazy circles around the tree, and so did his brothers and sisters. They zigged and zagged all day. They swooped and swerved. Jackson's ears stood straight up now.

He ran so wildly that they bobbed around on his head like they were out of joint.

With rabs, just as in many animals, this play is very important. For rabs save themselves by quick flight and an elusive course which the pursuer cannot follow. They run patterns very much like football players do. Jackson was very skilled in this. He would do a quick circle around the tree, fake a right hand turn, then jump left and hide under a bush making himself as flat as a newspaper, his ears way way back. Jackson could pour on the speed. He'd take off at one end of the yard and when he got going he was a white tornado, but always he had to stop at the other end just at a white gate.

Without asking, Jackson knew he was not supposed to go out of the yard, but he always wondered what lay beyond that gate. For him that gate was an obstacle to finding out what he was really made of. He hated to stop when he wasn't even tired. Jackson thought and thought but try as he might, his mind could not tell him what was behind that gate. Jackson's feet were so much bigger than his mind.

So, spring blossomed and the rabs happily cracked carrots, thumped on their box and chased each other around the tree. Jackson discovered that his oversized feet could dig up dirt, so he fell to making tunnels under the box. He scratched up the earth with his front paws and sent it flying a full yard in back of him with his powerful back feet. He was over two months old now and he dug in every corner and chewed every bush and branch. He was restless and the garden seemed to grow smaller all the time. Even without thinking, his huge hind feet would let go sending him high in the air. Jackson was like a coiled spring. The mom rabbit took very little interest in her children now.

Jackson could dig under the gate unnoticed and it was even easier than he thought. Just a little hole would do cuz rabs have a lot of fur and fat and they can squeeze through tiny places. When Jackson saw light at the other end of his tunnel, his heart raced. It was the first light he had ever seen from the outside. One last big push and he was out. There before him was not just one tree but many trees and many houses, and roads too, that you could run as long as you wanted. Jackson gave a few hops and he came to a square brick column with a lantern on it. Jackson was really on fire now. He was gonna bust loose. He was cock sure of himself. One giant leap and off he went, hop, hop, hop down the sidewalk.

The houses whizzed past. The wind blew through his ears and against his face. Hop, hop, hop, hop, He raced by an old lady planting seeds along a trellis. She straightened up in fear, but she never even saw him pass. Jackson laughed and laughed. He wasn't even tired. He just hopped for joy. Then he came to a railroad track. Hop, hop, hop, hop, hop. Next he came to a long wide street with cars. Hop, hop, hop, hop. Then he felt grass under his feet and stopped. He was in the middle of a large park. He had run farther and faster than ever before in his life.

He looked all around him and as far as he could see there was grass. He nibbled for awhile and then lay down to sleep under a safe bush. He slept for a long time, then some small instinct in him made him wake up with a start. Perhaps it was the drop in temperature or the strange darkness. When he looked up, the sun had disappeared behind the clouds which had bright fringes around the sides but dark, troubled centers. A breeze sent dried leaves scurrying around him. Then unfriendly gusts of wind blew up his back, matting his fur. It was growing cold and dark. Jackson's thoughts turned to home but his big feet had carried him so much farther than his little mind could remember. He didn't know which way to hop first. Jackson was lost, and for the first time, he was scared. When the first drops hit his nose, he high-tailed it for the biggest bush he could find. Then, all of a sudden, terrible claps of thunder rent the heavens open and water poured out soaking everything with its icy fingers. There was no snug upside down box he could call home, No where at all to hide. Another terrible roar of thunder sent Jackson running in panic right into a puddle. The poor baby rabbit struggled even to the point of swimming to escape. The lightning and thunder raged gleefully overhead at his plight. Jackson cried and cried cuz he never should have burrowed under that gate. He was sopping wet, numb and shaking all over from the cold.

After the heavens poured out all their water, the silver linings reappeared; it was over. The sun came out in all its majesty and touched each raindrop as it hung on the budding branches. Everything sparkled, but Jackson wailed and wailed. He would never see his brothers and sisters again! He took a deep breath so he could cry some more, but then he heard someone else crying not so far away. He was so astonished, that he stood quiet and still, listening to sobs and whimpers coming from a little clump of trees. And there behind the biggest tree Jackson saw the strangest sight a rabbit could see. There sat a huge white rabbit, twice his size in the middle of turned over baskets, their colored eggs spilled out on the wet ground. There were hundreds of baskets and thousands of eggs all over the ground. In the middle, propped against the tree was this old rabbit with a red bow tie crying over and over that the little children would not get their Easter eggs this year, cuz of the storm, and cuz he was so old. "Mr. Rabbit, I'll help you deliver your eggs," said Jackson who wanted the big rabbit to stop crying. He considered Jackson's little body and big feet. Then young and old offered suggestions about how the eggs could be saved.

So, Jackson put his big hind legs to work delivering eggs. He really worked hard. He loaded up baskets and hauled them up to front porches. Jackson could really haul the freight. The old rabbit gave directions and Jackson listened, trying hard to remember each detail. First, he delivered soft pastels and double dips to the children bordering the park, then he delivered hot pinks and blue and golds to families on streets that emptied into the park. He had burnt sienna for an Italian family and red lacquer for a Chinese family. He also gave away Scotch plaids and ginghams which were very hard to make. Then he crossed a wide street with lots of cars and delivered eggs with fluorescent colors.

Jackson had a good memory for details. You could say that his mind was catching up to his big feet. Next, he crossed a railroad track and dropped off sparkels and red, white and blues, placing them carefully by the door, but not where they would be stepped on. He sorted eggs in the daylight and hauled baskets into the night. The old rabbit was now very happy and talked about their plans for the future. Now Jackson's legs were tired cuz he had to haul the eggs longer distances. He delivered eggs with decals of the saints and of Jesus to the Mexican children. He delivered smiling faces and burgundies. To small, poor houses, Jackson gave his favorite eggs, chocolate block busters!

    He passed a house with a trellis and noticed sweet peas just growing up the wooden slats. They were in gay Easter colors too. Jackson was old enough now just to look and not to eat. He judged distances and made estimates on weight. Since he kept the same pace in his work day, he could plan his schedule weeks in advance. Adding and subtracting became easier.

The streets came together in his mind. Jackson hurried now cuz he was a half-hour late. He almost bumped into a brick post but kept on going. Then he turned around and looked at the lantern on top. Jackson wondered if he had seen it before. He studied it for a whole half minute. It was strange and yet familiar like an old toy out of his past. "I was here," Jackson said out loud. "I was here before." "I came by this lantern... from over there," and that's exactly where he headed. There was his old gate. He was home and he didn't even know it. There were his brothers and sisters cracking carrots, thumping on their box and running circles around the tree just like always.

Jackson lived happily ever after, and remember if your feet are too big, the rest of you will grow up too. Just forget your sorrow, pitch in and help and you'll find your way home.

www.ingramcontent.com/pod-product-compliance
Lightning Source LLC
LaVergne TN
LVHW070444070526
838199LV00036B/692

JACKSON

Meet Jackson, a curious young rabbit with oversized feet and an even bigger sense of adventure! Born in a cozy backyard nest, Jackson can't resist the call of the world beyond his gate. With each hop, he races through new thrills—until he finds himself lost in the big, wide world. But when an unexpected storm threatens to ruin Easter, Jackson steps up to help a wise old rabbit deliver baskets of colorful eggs to children everywhere. Will Jackson's big feet lead him back home? This delightful tale is packed with heart, humor, and the joy of discovering your true potential.

MARPLE'S
Arples

GEORGE; JUDY ENNIS